The Double Life of an

Alaskan Sled Dog

Written by

Andrea "Finney" Aufder Heyde

Edited by Larry Dale

Illustrated by Joe Lee

authorHOUSE®

AuthorHouse™
1663 Liberty Drive
Bloomington, IN 47403
www.authorhouse.com
Phone: 1-800-839-8640

Published by AuthorHouse 1/10/2012

ISBN: 978-1-4685-3793-2 (e)
ISBN: 978-1-4685-3794-9 (sc)

Library of Congress Control Number: 2011963730

Contents

Preface

Andrea Aufder Heyde has been known as Finney during her thirty-four years in her teaching profession. Because of her passion for teaching her students about Alaska and the Iditarod Sled Dog Race, she enthusiastically embraced her school's adoption of a program called CLASS (Connecting Learning Assures Successful Students), which focused on setting goals and using life skills to achieve the goals. In doing so she was inspired to contact the Iditarod education department and shared with them her idea of being a teacher who would go out on the Iditarod Trail and send messages back citing how life skills were being used by not only the mushers, drivers of the sleds, but the dogs to achieve their goal of going from Anchorage to Nome. After steadfastly believing in the educational value of her idea and using many of the life skills herself, the Iditarod committee finally agreed that her idea had value and she could be the first Teacher on the Trail in 1999. She was flown by bush planes as close to most of the checkpoints as possible and dropped off to hike her way to the villages. There she excitedly and passionately watched, listened, and learned the ins and outs of the race, viewed excellent dog care, and interacted with the extraordinary village natives, Iditarod volunteers, teachers, and bush pilots.

After her trail experience she felt she needed to teach her students about the raising and training of the sled dogs, so she asked a musher if she could work at her Iditarod kennel for a summer. That summer turned into many, many summers of constant hands-on experience with the training and running of a kennel. It was eye opening and constantly gave her more to teach her students. Annui's story began the first summer at the kennel when Finney met the litter of wee babies. On the flight home to Indiana with Annui in a little cat crate under the seat of the plane, Finney began to write Annui's story. It has developed over the years, and Finney felt passionate about telling Annui's story as a tribute to her devotion and love. Many years and adventures have gone by, and the story has now been told. Annui is telling her story, and all the events in the story are true.

Annui just turned twelve years old and still has the urge to run and pull, but the running is not as fast and the pulling not as strong. She has led an incredible life, and Finney feels very fortunate to have been given her the summer of 1999. They both simply can't wait for cold weather to arrive and for snowflakes to fall. They both become feistier and their steps are quicker and lighter. Their hearts are intertwined in many, many ways. Finney salutes the ease with which Annui embraced her double life. She is one in a million, and her story is worth being told!

Acknowledgments

A huge thank you is sent to my family, dear friends, teachers, and students who "listened" to my story again and again and encouraged me to write it! Annui and I have a bond that will be forever, and I feel I am simply the "musher," as she takes me along on her journey of *The Double Life of an Alaskan Sled Dog*. I also look forward to the little "Brat" Soofie continuing to be a part of this journey!

I also send out a special thanks to Nancy Martin who captured the perfect front cover and back cover photograph.

Thanks, Finney

Chapter 1
Life with My Family in Alaska

I was born on June 21 in an Alaskan Iditarod sled dog kennel. That is a place where dogs live and train to run the famous Iditarod Sled Dog Race. It is known as "The Last Great Race on Earth" and goes from Anchorage to Nome, Alaska, which is over a thousand miles long. I had four brothers, and although we all had the same birthday, my brothers were much, much bigger and much, much stronger. I loved them all but I felt lonely because most of the time they played with each other and not me because I was truly the *little* sister. My brothers could be rough and feisty. I tried my very hardest to keep up with them and to not cry out when they accidentally hurt me. I secretly wished there might be someone who could help me with my rambunctious brothers. We were all little husky fur babies known as Alaskan sled dogs.

Being wee puppies we lived in a house above the ground with a long wire area behind it in which we would run and romp. It was like a screened-in porch. The house part had straw in it to sleep on, and our food was kept there, too. In the wire area, we could run, play, roll around on each other, and always get a fresh, cool drink of water. Since it was like a playground, we played with our chewy toys and balls. I especially liked the toys since I usually played by myself. Our mother, whose name was Topaz, would still spend the nights with us to keep us cozy and warm and then only part of the day. She soon began to spend entire days at her own house nearby. The time away from us allowed her to begin looking forward to running with the team of dogs again and to get her body back in shape. She, like all the other dogs, was happy and healthy. Our father, Sandman, was an incredibly smart sled dog who had run the Iditarod race and many other races. He helped train pups like us. Everyone hoped we'd all become super race dogs. I sometimes wondered if that would happen to me when I grew up. It was nice to dream about during my many naps.

When we were three weeks old a summer helper who was living at the kennel, which is a place where a group of dogs live, began to take care of us. Every day the helper would put fresh straw in our house. She made certain there was always plenty of dry food and clean water for us, and she scrubbed the wire cage until it sparkled. It didn't take long for the helper to fall in love with me because I tried my best to always get her attention. I sat quietly and turned my head in every possible direction so I could watch her while she worked. When I stood up I wagged my tail so hard it would make me take a nosedive. She would look at me, grin big, and laugh out loud. The helper couldn't play with us when she worked, but when she finished she would always give us hugs. I seemed to be hugged longer and harder than my brothers!

Since the helper was spending so much time caring for us, she was told by the kennel owner that she could name us. The helper began with my brothers. She thought of names for them because of their coloring and personalities. One of my brothers was brown and black with a little white, so she named him Freckles; one was a light brown with a white tummy, so she named him Sandy; one was always wagging his tail, so she named him Happy; and one was all white like our mom, so she named him Snow. Snow was adopted very early on by a family from Germany that visited the kennel. They immediately named him Balto after a *very* famous sled dog. Finally, it was my turn to be named. I knew she would give me a really special name, so I was surprised and a little disappointed when I heard her name me "Sissy." Oh, how could she do that? I am not a sissy! I am not rough like my brothers, but I am *not* a sissy. The helper reached out to pick me up, and I turned and ran away from her. She had hurt my feelings naming me Sissy, and I wanted her to know how I was feeling. The helper had come to know me quite well, so when I ran away she knew I was unhappy. "Aw, Sissy," she said. "I didn't name you Sissy to make fun of you. It is just a short and loving name for "Sister." You are your brothers' precious little sister and should have that name." I guess sometimes when you don't understand something you get your feelings hurt, just like I did. When I finally stopped and listened to the helper, I realized she was just being kind. I saw the helper still had her hands outstretched and open, waiting for me. I ran as fast as my little legs would go and jumped into her hands so she could pick me up and give me a hug, which certainly made me feel so much better!

The helper took care of my brothers and me all summer long. Whenever she had extra time from all her kennel jobs she would come to our house and spend time with us. The helper loved us all, but I knew by the look in her eyes that she loved me just a tiny bit more. My brothers and I learned to trust the helper. We knew that she would always give us the best care and make certain we were all happy and doing well. Even though we still had our furry mother, the helper had become like our mom too, only she was a human.

One day the musher, who is the driver of the sled and who happens to be the owner of the kennel, told the helper that she had been watching how well she cared for us. She said she knew the helper had a special place in her heart for me. The musher told her that when she left the kennel and went back to her home in the lower forty-eight, she could take me with her. *But,* she couldn't take a sled dog from an Iditarod kennel in Alaska with the name Sissy. She told the helper that people would not know that she had four brothers or that the name Sissy was a short and loving name for sister. She told her she would have to find another name for me. That night the helper found the word Aniu, (ah-nee-OO) which is an Inupiaq Eskimo word meaning falling snow. The helper changed the spelling a little bit and decided to name me, Annui (ah-noo-EE), which she thought was a very fancy name. I was quite happy to learn why my name had been changed and what my fancy new name meant, but then the helper had more news for me. She told me she soon had to leave the kennel and go back to her home to teach school. Quite suddenly a feeling of great sadness came over me at the thought of the helper leaving the kennel. I loved her and wanted her to stay with us forever. She then told me that the musher said she could take me with her. I could hardly believe the news and became so excited I found myself jumping and running around in circles. Then it suddenly hit me. I would have to leave my rascally brothers, who I really did love, and my mother and my father, both whom I dearly, dearly loved. How would I be able to leave them all behind? I was just six weeks old and had only ever lived with my brothers and our mom and dad at the kennel. How would I be able to go so far away from them? I knew I would miss my family. What was I to do, and could I actually leave my family?

After thinking it over and sleeping on it for a couple of nights,

I finally decided that since I truly trusted and loved the helper, I had to believe that leaving my family in Alaska would be a good thing for me. I also realized that the helper would now become my owner, caring for only me. I knew how much Topaz and Sandman loved me, as well as my silly but fun brothers, and now I had to believe the same of my new owner.

On a Saturday morning in August, after spending one last night with my mother, father, and brothers, I flew out of Alaska with my owner, and I headed to my new home many, many miles and hours away in Indiana. It may be hard to understand, as I was a bit sad yet also happy to begin this exciting journey. My owner promised we would return to the kennel in Alaska to see my family once again. I knew I could believe her. I left with tears in my eyes but with happiness and excitement in my heart, ready to begin whatever lay ahead. I didn't have a clue about the life I was about to lead, but the one thing I did know was that my owner and I would lead it together!

Chapter II
My Days at School

After settling into my new home, I began going to a school for children when I was only three months old. This was because my owner, who I now decided to call mom, was a teacher and went to school every day. Since I was so young, Mom didn't want to leave me home alone. I was quite curious about meeting all those human creatures who would be in my classroom. I was a little afraid and nervous about this new adventure, but I wanted to be there with my mom and not home all by myself. The first day of school arrived, and the strange creatures entered my schoolroom. I was so excited that all I could do was run from one to the other checking to see if they had dog or cat smells on them. I was amazed at how big they were, but it might have only seemed that way because I was still so little. Even though I was delighted to be there, it took courage for me to be around that many little creatures with so many hands and feet! I learned that the strange friends were actually wonderful children who adored having me with them in their classroom.

Every day when I arrived at school, I would wait patiently while Mom organized the children's work for the day and put fresh water in my very own drinking bowl. Then we would go outside into a fenced courtyard to exercise and get my wiggles out so I could be settled in the classroom. Sometimes, if I was really lucky, children who were at school a little early would come outside and play with me. I would fetch balls or a Frisbee, race through the gardens, and occasionally splash into the pond! Returning to the classroom, I eagerly awaited the arrival of my classmates. Seeing them caused me to whine and cry for joy. I soon realized that the classroom was filled with loving friends. I was young and losing my baby teeth, just like my classmates, and I liked to chew on everything I could find on the floor. My friends in the room always remembered to pick up erasers, pencils, crayons, and paper. They cared a lot about me and didn't want me to get a tummy ache.

A rule in my classroom was, if you work during work time you could play during playtime, which was really recess. Since I wanted to play with everyone during playtime, I would go into the crate that my mom had brought to school and nap during work time. I knew that it would not be a good thing to disturb anyone, and that if I did, I might have to stay at home. Anyway, I really needed the nap time because I was still very young, and tired easily! Playtime was always such fun, not only for me, but for my classmates too. No one ever wanted to miss it.

In the fall, winter, and spring, my friends and I would go into the fenced courtyard during recess to play a rousing game of soccer. My favorite time of the year for soccer was winter when there was a fresh coating of snow on the ground, and the air was crispy cold. I am certain winter was my very favorite season because of the Alaskan blood in me! I felt deliriously happy and had a smile on my face as I raced, jumped, and tumbled. My classmates wanted me to be on their team because I was very fast, and because I could even do headers with the soccer ball.

But I liked being my own team! I loved playing against the entire class. I would grab the soccer ball in my mouth, run the length of the courtyard, and leave everyone behind as they scrambled to catch me. It was such fun being the "*star*"! The soccer games always seemed to end too quickly. Playtime was over, and it was back into the classroom for all of us.

I really liked going to school with Mom. It was fun to be with my mom and my friends every day. I always got the warmest hugs, with a few kisses thrown in, making me purr. Yes, I do purr, but it is a doggie purr *not* a cat purr. Cats sound like they have a motor. I make my purr sound deep in my throat. My mom loves it when I purr for her because she knows I must be really happy. I seemed to be doing a lot of purring, especially the nights after being at school. I didn't think I could ever be any happier!

Chapter III
Growing Up Can Be Challenging

As I grew bigger, Mom was determined that a big dog should be a well-behaved dog. There was no way around it. Whether I liked it or not, I was headed to a school for dogs called canine school. Being a sled dog, I loved to run and pull, so when Mom hooked me on my lead for a walk, I did the natural thing for me to do, and that was to pull her along. I had a feeling that was going to change! I knew it would be very hard for me to learn *not* to do, but I had no idea that there might be something else almost as hard.

On my first day of canine school I met about twenty other dogs, and I thought it would be super fun to play chase with all of them. I had to quickly remember Mom's classroom rule of working during work time so that I could play during playtime. I found this extremely difficult to do at canine school, because I wanted to romp and play with all my furry friends. During the teaching time I took my work quite seriously. Since they had breaks for playing, I always worked hard, eagerly looking forward to the breaks, which were like the recess in the classroom! I knew I was a good student, and I found the obedience commands such as sit, down, stay, and heel to be easy to learn. But my, oh my, I had no idea how hard learning the command "come" would be! It meant I would have to stop and "come" even when I was having such a good time sniffing around in my yard, digging a deep hole in a garden, chewing on an old smelly shoe or deliciously dirty bone, and even if I was napping. I adored my mom, but I didn't always want to stop what I was doing to go to her when she said the "come" command. I learned all the other commands quickly, but it seemed I needed extra help with "come." I had to go to two sessions of regular canine school. And I must confess something to you, I was not always the *perfect* student!

Yours truly had to go to Saturday school! This was kind of like being sent to the principal's office but on the weekend. It was not fun, and I was terribly embarrassed. I am certain you already know the command that got me into trouble. Yes, indeed, it was *"come."* But truthfully it was not the command that got me into trouble but my behavior when I heard it. I chose to continue doing what I wanted to do and pretended I did not hear my mom or anyone else say, "Come, Annui, come." That's how I landed myself in Saturday school one frigid, cold morning in winter.

Mom, the canine school teacher, and I met at a huge park. I went over and over and *over* what I needed to do when I heard, *"Come."* I had to be hooked to a very long lead that let me run far away from Mom. Then when she said *"come,"* I had to turn and run back to her right away. If I didn't turn and move toward her she would say *"come"* again and then quickly pull the long lead toward her. That would certainly make me run at an amazing speed in her direction! When I did what she asked me to do, she would give me a yummy treat and tell me, "Good come." If I was hesitant in my *"come,"* no treat!

It took two hours until I finally got it right every time. Sometimes I found a very interesting smell, saw another dog, totally ignored my mom, or I simply chose to not listen. When I didn't turn to go toward Mom as soon as she said *"come,"* that was not a good thing. She never yelled at me, but I didn't see a smile on her face. Then we had to do it again and again! I decided to really start paying attention and listening because even I was getting a bit cold, and snow had begun to fall. So, as soon as I heard *"come"* I turned *immediately* and went zooming toward my mom. We practiced it maybe five more times, and the teacher finally said he was pleased that I had settled down and focused on learning the command. Mom thanked the teacher, said good-bye, and we drove home cold and snow-covered but happy. And, guess what, I *never* went to Saturday school again!

I graduated from canine school and had my picture taken with my mom and my classmates. I received a graduation certificate with my fancy name on it, and in big letters it said I had learned the very important command *"come"* … but only after attending Saturday school! I learned to pay attention to Mom by listening to her voice and watching her. I even learned to do the commands when Mom used hand signals and not her voice. I loved to see the smile on her face and hear the loving words she always used when we did the commands together.

Another hard task was to remember not to pull when I was hooked to the lead. Sometimes I couldn't understand why I had to walk nicely beside Mom when she knew how in my heart I was born to pull. Since I loved to run too, a very nice thing Mom always did was to let me run free in an open field after we had a good walk. I felt the running free was my reward for not pulling, so I really concentrated hard to walk slowly like a *very* well-behaved dog. How I loved the freedom of running and leaping as I felt the wind on my face and ears. I loved stretching out my legs so far that it almost felt like I was flying. Something inside seemed to tell me that this was the way a sled dog should feel when running hooked to a sled. While I was having such a wonderful time, I always made certain to check where my mom was and to listen for the obedience command I had struggled with … *"Come!"* When I heard it, I would race to her with my tail held high and a grin on my face. I really loved to hold my tail high and grin! I would sit and wait for Mom to hook the lead to my collar once again, and then we would happily walk home together.

I had the best year ever going to school with my mom and being with all the friends in our classroom. I enjoyed going to canine school to learn how to be a well-behaved sled dog because I knew that was important to my mom. The school year was coming to an end soon, and I wondered if mom would remember she had promised to take me back to Alaska to see my family. I knew my mother and father would be so proud of all I had learned, and maybe my brothers would see how special I had become. I felt quite lucky to have been chosen to live a whole different life in Indiana.

After all my challenging work at the canine school, learning the obedience commands and learning not to pull when hooked on a lead, I knew my mom thought I was the smartest and greatest dog ever! We had become the best of friends, caring for each other, being loyal, and trusting each other. What could be better than that? Maybe, just maybe, a return trip to Alaska to see my family once again!

Chapter IV
My Adventurous Return to Alaska

All my schools were over, and I began to wonder if my mom would keep the promise she had made about returning to Alaska. It wasn't long into the summer vacation when I noticed her hauling out a huge suitcase and backpack. I remembered that same suitcase from our first flight to our home, so I knew Mom was probably going to do some traveling. I was hoping it would be to Alaska and that I would make the trip with her. But gosh, I didn't see any of my doggie things being packed. Maybe she was waiting until right before we were to leave to pack my things. I knew in my heart that she would keep her word, but I needed some sort of a sign to be certain that we were going to travel together.

One day my mom took me to my veterinarian, who I felt very safe with and who always kept me feeling well. It seemed I had to have some shots and some papers filled out by the doctor and Mom. I heard the doctor and her talking about me traveling in the belly of an airplane but that I'd have to be inside a crate. Oh, boy, was I really going to go back to see my family? I decided I should listen very carefully to all that was being said! The veterinarian told my mom to freeze water in little paper cups and to put them in the crate with me, to make certain I had plenty of water. I could lick them when I was thirsty, and they would stay frozen a long time, since it was always cold in the belly of a plane. I heard them say it would be a long flight but that Mom could get me out of the plane at the stop in the Saint Paul-Minneapolis Airport, where we had to switch to another plane. We could spend some time together and get exercise by walking around in a special area they have for dogs. The next part of the trip, from Saint Paul-Minneapolis Airport to Anchorage, Alaska, would be the longest, but seeing my mom for an hour would make the trip much easier for me.

The day arrived to leave, and we got up quite early in the morning. Mom loaded the crate into the car and crammed in all our bags; I hopped into my favorite spot in the car and off we headed to the Indianapolis Airport. I had to stay in the crate at the airport while Mom checked us in for the flights. People kept going by the crate and would "oooh and aaah" when they saw me. I was behaving very nicely and was resting with my nose against the crate's door. I was just beginning to get butterflies in my tummy when Mom came back.

She seemed to sense that I was a little unsettled, maybe because my nose was pressed very tightly against the door and my eyes were open quite wide as I looked in every direction! She spoke calmly and quietly, which made me feel so much better.

We finally had to leave each other, and that was hard for both of us. I could tell by my mom's watery eyes that she was already missing me, and I honestly wasn't thrilled about this new adventure of flying in a crate all by myself. At least when I flew with my mom as a baby, I was able to be on the plane with her in a very small carry-on crate. Now that I was a year old, I had to fly in the belly of the plane all by myself. Mom and I had never been apart since we returned to her home, so this was very scary for both of us.

We met again at the Saint Paul-Minneapolis Airport, and I was simply overjoyed to see her. That part of the flight trip had gone well, and I noticed there were a couple of other crates near mine with dogs inside them. They did not seem the least bit frightened, and none of the dogs made one sound, not a yip, yap, or yup! They just curled up and tried to sleep or rest. During this break in the long flight, Mom and I had time to exercise, drink water, and, most importantly, be together. I thought Mom was holding me a little tighter than usual, kissing me more than usual, and talking to me nonstop. She always talked to me, but not this much! I certainly felt loved, and I really was okay because everything had gone smoothly on the first part of the trip. I actually was getting a wee bit excited, for I knew that in about eight hours I would see my family again. I began to wonder how my fur parents would feel about how big I'd gotten. I wondered if my brothers would be much bigger than I was and what it would be like to be with them again. What would they think of me now?

It was time for Mom to put me back into the crate and take it to the place where dogs had to be checked in. She hugged and kissed me good-bye again, and I gave her a big, wet lick. I was quite content to curl up and take a nap, as I knew I would probably dream about my return to the kennel. I couldn't wait to see the reaction of my family when they saw me! Even though I had learned so much in one year, I was looking forward to a summer of learning new things at the kennel. Having spent a year with my mom in her part of the world, it was now time to go back to my part of the world and learn what life is really like in an Alaskan Iditarod sled dog kennel. Little did I know that this one-year-old sled dog was on her way to living what might later be known as a double life!

Chapter V
Family Reunion and More

I was back where I was born, but now it was all so different. I was no longer a wee baby, but a yearling. My mom was a little afraid that all the dogs at the kennel would frighten me, so she kept me with her in the bunkhouse, which is a place for the workers to sleep while working at the kennel. I had to become used to all the barking and howling, and since there were about eighty dogs it was quite loud at times. Dogs were being trained to race; dogs had all kinds of trail experience, and dogs were of all ages. I had no idea where my brothers, were but I knew they were sitting on their doghouses some place in the kennel. I hadn't been able to see my family yet because I needed to feel a bit more confident about being with so many dogs. When Mom worked during the day, she attached me to a long chain that was then attached to a pole in front of my doghouse. I could sit on my house, stay in the house, or walk all around the house. I always had fresh water and a clean area to walk around. Mom told me it would be a few days before I would be able to go see my family. She had already seen my brothers and my father, and told me they were eager to see me. I learned that my mother had left the kennel and was staying with another family. That made me sad at first, but I realized my mother, Topaz, was being taken care of because she had retired from being a racing sled dog. Now she would be a pet sled dog for the rest of her life.

One morning, quite unexpectedly, Mom moved me to a doghouse that was surrounded by other doghouses. I knew it was time for me to become a real part of the kennel. The plan was for me to stay at the doghouse all day and then go back to the bunkhouse with her at the end of her workday. I thought about how nice it would be to sleep on a soft bed indoors, at least for a little while longer! Yes, in the bunkhouse I slept on Mom's bed or on a couch, but of course I was not one bit spoiled!

I had no idea that this would turn out to be such a special day. My mom told me that I was *finally* going to meet my brothers. She said they immediately remembered her and had been absolutely crazy with happiness to see her again. Now it was time for them to see their little sister all grown up and well trained. Off we went. My brothers were indeed amazed when they saw me, for I was now a beautiful gray, white, and sand color.

I had a long elegant, neck; shapely, muscular legs; pointed, intelligent ears; and short black fur that stood up to make a ridge that ran up my nose. Mom said I had what looked like a Mohawk running up my nose and between my eyes! I had beautiful, curious yellow wolf eyes and an air of great confidence. My brothers were astounded. Their mouths dropped open, and then they fell all over themselves trying to get my attention. I simply stood there and looked at them as they jumped, ran, and acted much like they did when they were puppies. I knew I had grown up, but I wondered about my brothers.

Then it was time to go see my father, Sandman. He had become one of the best sled dogs at the kennel, beside my famous grandfather, Argie, who was the patriarch, or the honored father, of the entire kennel. As Mom and I approached Sandman, he began walking back and forth, wagging his tail and whining. There was no doubt that Sandman was my father, for I do the same whining when I am happy and when I greet a friend, fur or human. All the dogs stopped and watched as Sandman and I "talked," then we sniffed each other all over, and finally we just stood together with our bodies leaning into one another. How happy we both were to be together again! Soon we decided to lie down and rest, and Mom was totally shocked at what she saw.

When Sandman was down on his tummy he crossed his front legs; when she looked over at me, there I was on my tummy with my front legs crossed also. She turned and looked over at my grandfather Argie, who was resting nearby, and he too had his front legs crossed. It certainly was a family trait, and even though I had been away from them for the first year of my life, I had inherited the same habit as my father and grandfather. It felt so good to be with my father again and I didn't know it at the time, but I was destined to spend a great deal of time with him that summer.

I began thinking about this return visit and wondering what might happen while I was at the kennel. Maybe I was back at the kennel to learn how to be a racing sled dog like my mother, father, and grandfather. Maybe I would be trail trained with my brothers, because I knew they would eventually race in the Iditarod Sled Dog Race. I realized that all the dogs surrounding me were older dogs and had already run in the Iditarod or were my age and were training to run in it. It seemed like it might be back to school again, but this time I was in Alaska at an Iditarod sled dog kennel with my family. Maybe we were all going to be part of an Iditarod training school!

Chapter VI
Iditarod Training Begins

Because I was now spending my days with all the other sled dogs, I felt like one of them. I ate breakfast and played with them, and looked forward to Mom working around my house and the area where I stayed. My brothers and father were sitting on houses nearby, so it felt like a family affair! I don't tell this very often because I don't want you to think I am a "sissy," but I continued to go back to the bunkhouse at night with Mom to sleep on her soft bed or the couch!

It didn't take long for the Iditarod training school to begin. The first thing I had to get used to was the feel of the harness on my back. I needed to have the right size so that it wouldn't be too tight and rub or too loose and bother me when I ran. I also had to have a slip-on collar so that when I was hooked to the gangline, the main line all the dogs are attached to, it wouldn't break or snap apart when I pulled. My mom tried to buy a slip collar at a feed store, and the only collar they had left in my size was bright pink. Since I have a very long neck, when I sat on top of my house I knew the bright pink slip collar would really stand out. I was a little concerned that my brothers would remember my baby name of Sissy and start teasing me because of the pink, pink, *pink* collar.

Mom told me that it looked lovely. Since I wanted to prove to my brothers that I could be an Iditarod trained sled dog, I knew the pink collar wasn't going to help convince them. I hoped that maybe later on my mom would go back to the feed store and see if she could find another color, blue, red, purple or black, but not pink! Eventually I did get a lovely blue slip collar that matched my harness and lead.

The next thing my brothers and I had to learn after tolerating the harness was to be patient after being hooked to the gangline. It took time to hook everybody up, so learning to wait and not fool around was a big deal. I eventually learned that I was always going to be hooked on the left side of the gangline. There was a good reason for that and I will explain. When I went to canine school I had to do all the obedience commands on Mom's left side. So that made the left side of the gangline the most comfortable for me. If I was on the right side I always wanted to push into my partner on the left side. Nobody was very happy when I did that! So my partner was always on the right side of the gangline, and I was on the left, just like a left-handed person.

After my harness was put over my head and then my front legs were put though, I was hooked from my collar to the neckline, which is a rope extending from the gangline. The tugline, which extends from the gangline, was attached to the tug. The tug was a small loop of rope at the end of my harness. From the neckline to the tugline was my space in which I ran. It was a great temptation to chew on the gangline while all the other dogs were being attached. *I* never did that. But I saw my brothers being naughty and trying to chew.

Now we were all single file attached to the gangline, and I was in the middle of my brothers. We were to be standing quietly and behaving ourselves. Our father, Sandman, did turn around to eye my brothers, which really didn't stop them from chewing or fussing. Even though they were "eyed" by their father, they continued to misbehave. Boys will be boys!

The gangline was attached to a four-wheeled motorized vehicle, called a "four-wheeler." It was summer, so we trained with it because there was no snow on the ground. We were all single file in a line just like we would have been if we had been attached to a sled but without a partner. After all of us had stopped barking, the musher, who was the driver of the sled, or in this case the four-wheeler, walked back to the four-wheeler and got on. After Mom got on, the musher started the engine and said quietly, "All righty, then." Sandman leaped into the air as he pulled as hard as he could. *Yikes!* I felt myself being tugged forward by the neckline, so I trotted ahead. Then I was pulled backward by the tugline. I slowed down. It took me a while to figure out how to run in my space so that I wasn't pulled forward and backwards, forward and backwards.

The musher turned to my mom and told her that she could see I wasn't afraid to try new things. I was so happy to hear that because I truly wasn't certain about what was happening to me. I was a little scared! The musher then told Mom that the *big* test for me would come later on the trail, after we had gone up and down some hills and around some curves. I wish I hadn't overheard that because it made me wonder what the *big* test was going to be. We all just trotted on, keeping the lines tight as we pulled up and down the hills. If the musher wanted us to go a little faster she would gun the engine of the four-wheeler, but she kept us mostly in a trot, not a run. I looked ahead on a short straight part of the trail, and I saw a dip and then a huge metal tunnel called a culvert. It looked like we had to run down into it and out the other side. That had to be my *big* test! I kept trotting along and went down the dip; when the front of the team went into the culvert I never broke my stride but trotted right into it too. I was pretty proud of myself because I wasn't frightened at all and had decided to give every part of this new experience my best effort.

After all the dogs were inside the culvert the musher stopped the four-wheeler. She got off to pet all the dogs and to tell us we were such good dogs! She also gave us all a little treat, especially my brothers and me. We rested inside for a while because it was nice and cool, and felt good on our bellies. When the musher got back on to the four-wheeler, she turned to my mom and told her that I was a *"star"* because I had not slowed down or dragged my feet while going into the culvert. It looked like I had not been one bit afraid, but the truth was that I really was! The musher also said that I had been very well-trained and behaved perfectly when hooked to the gangline. She knew I would absolutely, positively, learn to be an Iditarod sled dog that summer. Mom and I both had grins on our faces as big as an Iditarod mile!!

When we finally returned to the kennel, I had a little drink of water to thin my saliva, which had gotten thick from pulling and trotting. I cooled myself down and rested on the ground while all the other dogs were taken back to their doghouses. I saw the look of pride in my brothers' eyes, because they realized I wasn't afraid of trying something new. I had used courage to simply trot into the culvert, just as they had done. None of us had energy to bark, much less whine. I knew they were already looking forward to early-morning runs, just as I was. We were all beginning to learn to be real sled dogs, and everyone seemed quite happy with their first run on the trails in the woods.

Now it was time to drink more water, rest, have a snack, and rest some more. As we rested I knew we would be rethinking our first trail run and eagerly anticipating more adventures. I wondered if I would ever be put in the lead position or whether I would remain a wheel, team, or swing dog. I thought that learning to be a lead dog would be quite a challenge. I was ready for it! But I wondered who would teach me. The kennel had many trained lead dogs, so maybe it would be one of them. *Or* would it be my father, Sandman?

Chapter VII
I Knew I Could Do It

My mom and I arrived at the dog lot early one morning when the air was still very chilly. She had on her work gloves, a warm fleece hat and jacket, long pants, and hiking boots. I had spent the night with Mom in the bunkhouse, so I was hooked to a lead and trotted alongside the four-wheeler as she drove it into the dog lot. Mom parked on the trail, got the gangline out, to which she would hook up eight dogs, and hooked it to the front of her four-wheeler. She chained the front of the gangline to a stake that was deep in the ground. It had two long chains coming off it for a very good reason. The lead dogs were attached to these while the other dogs were hooked up. They weren't supposed to turn around and walk into the team, because eventually the whole team would be turned around. Sandman never needed to be hooked to the chain because he knew the stay command and faced front, although he might look around at some of the yearlings and give them the "eye." Then Mom cleaned up around all the dogs' houses. She knew that shortly the musher would be coming to the dog lot and would choose the dogs that were going on the morning's run. I wondered if I would be chosen to run, if I would have a partner, and if my girlfriend Wanda would be my partner. Would I be in wheel, which is right in front of the four-wheeler; swing, which is right behind the leaders; team, where most of the dogs run; or lead, which is in the very front?

The musher arrived, and she started telling Mom which dogs she should harness and hook on the gangline. She wanted my brothers Happy and Sandy to be hooked up as partners; Freckles was to be with a dog named Annie. I could hardly breathe as I tried to wait patiently. *Finally* I heard my name mentioned. I was told I was to run in wheel position with Wanda. I was glad to have Wanda as a partner. She was a little older than I was and had already run in the Iditarod. Wanda lived in a doghouse right beside the one I stayed in during the day, and we often played together. She was always very kind and gentle with me even though she was bigger and older.

The musher told Mom to hook Sandman in lead with his brother AJ. After everyone was harnessed and hooked to the gangline, the team settled down as my mom and the musher sat on some of the now empty doghouses waiting for everyone to become quiet. This was a rule we had to learn at the kennel when we were training. Everyone on the gangline had to be quiet and calm before we could leave the kennel to run on the trails.

Soon the musher walked over to the four-wheeler. Mom unhooked the leader AJ, who was chained to the stake on the trail. She gave my father, the other lead dog, a gentle rub on his head as he was standing and facing straight ahead just as he should. I kept my eyes fastened on my mom. I watched as she walked toward the four-wheeler and then climbed up onto the back of it. The musher had turned on the engine, released the brakes, and quietly said, "All righty, then." I couldn't believe the excitement! Dogs were leaping into the air while lunging forward, all the while making barking or whining noises. The first time we ran,

I think all of us were a little too scared to do this jumping and barking thing. This was maybe our third run, and we were all feeling much more confident. I was ready to go, but I was still so very new at this whole idea of sled dog training, I was not quite as excited as the others and again just a wee bit scared. Of course I was not going to let my brothers see any fear in my eyes, but I knew Wanda understood my feelings.

We shot out of the kennel leaving howling dogs behind. They hadn't been picked to go! The trail was hilly and curvy, with other trails coming into it and going out from it. One spot on the trail had a huge pool of water that was fed by a spring running down from the mountains. The water was freezing! In the summer this was a good spot to stop and cool off, as the water came almost up to our bellies. This was part of the training. If we learned to have fun going through the water, then we wouldn't mind going through overflow, water which is on top of the frozen rivers. The first time I went into the water I walked in slowly and cautiously. It was so cold I actually gasped and shuddered, as it took my breath away. I realized that this was just a touch of the coldness that my brothers would encounter during the Iditarod race. I also knew it was important that I learn to relax and to play in the big pool of water just like all the other dogs.

On this training run, the musher stopped the team in a very woodsy area. She told my mom to unhook me and said she was going to unhook AJ. The musher wanted to switch our positions. Oh, my, I couldn't believe what was happening! My mom took me to the front of the gangline and hooked my tug to the tugline and then my collar to Sandman's neckline. My brothers were astounded when I walked by them trying to act very brave and confident. I was going to be running in lead with my father! Sandman was going to teach and train me to be a lead dog. *Wow!*

After hooking me up on the left side, Mom whispered to me that she knew I would be fine and to just let my father teach me. The switch was made, and on we went. I was simply amazed that I was actually running beside my father.

All went well on the straight and curvy trail, but then I heard the musher say in a high voice, "Gee, gee," because there was a fork in the trail. Before I knew it, I had become airborne with my legs running on nothing but air! I had suddenly been forced to run really, really fast, and too fast for my feet to stay on the ground. Sandman was pulling me by my neckline, and we were headed down the trail that veered to the right. I struggled to regain my footing and to catch my breath when my father looked over to see if I was okay. I was trotting once again right beside him. He then gave me a sled dog high five by raising his eyebrows up and down. I had done a "gee, gee" and now knew that it meant to take the team to the right. We continued on down the trail, and then we came to another fork. As we approached I was listening to hear what the musher would say, and all of a sudden I heard a high voiced, "Gee, gee." I knew exactly what to do. This time my father didn't have to slam into me for I quickly went to the right, pulling the dogs behind with me. Sandman was there beside me going the same way. He gave me another sled dog high five, and my heart swelled with joy.

Again we continued up, down, and around curves on the trail, all trotting along nicely. In the distance I saw another fork in the trail. I was listening for the high "gee, gee," but as we were almost to the fork I heard, "Haw, haw," in a lower voice. Sandman immediately slammed into my side, pushing me off to the left. I thought I was going to lose my balance, but I somehow got my legs steadied under me and quickly kept on trotting as I went onto the trail on the left. This time I didn't get the sled dog high five. I was a little disappointed but realized that if I were hooked on the left side of the gangline in lead position and if I were given the low voice "haw, haw" command, I had better be ready to trot a lot faster to help the team turn left. Being hooked on the right side of the gangline and turning right was a lot easier. What a way to learn all these new trail commands!

On the way into the kennel the musher had us do two more "haw, haws," which I was eager to practice. By the time I did the second turn to the left, Sandman gave me a *big* sled dog high-five, because he knew I was really trying hard. This was my very first experience being a lead dog! He was so proud of me and knew I desperately wanted to learn how to be a racing sled dog. That made him very happy. He seemed delighted to be my teacher and sincerely wanted me to learn. That way I could run either with him in lead or as a swing, team, or wheel dog.

Sandman and I brought the team back to the kennel, and everyone was happy with the practice run. The musher thought I had learned quickly. Sandman was extremely thrilled to be teaching me, his only daughter. My brothers were in awe of how well their little sister had done. My mom, who had known all along that I would do just fine, had a silly grin on her face! It was a great day for everyone, but especially for me. I had been trained to be a lead dog. *Wow!* I knew I would need more practice, but I was ready. Now I knew exactly why I had come back to the kennel. It was not only to visit with my family again, but to be trained by my father, Sandman, to be a lead dog. Was I ever a very, very lucky sled dog!

My summer at the kennel continued with me running lead with my father in front of a four-wheeler and learning how to pull a sled on grass. I had to get used to the weight of the sled behind me, and I had to listen for the "gee"/"haw" commands and the "straight ahead" command. I also learned that "easy, easy" meant I needed to slow down. When I heard "whoa," I needed to stop immediately. Mom made plans to bring the sled back to Indiana so that we could go "mushing" during our snowy winters.

The summer seemed to fly by, and sure enough it was soon time to say good-bye again to my fur family and head home with Mom. I had worked hard and had learned an incredible amount about being a real Iditarod sled dog. I certainly knew how to pull, because I just naturally wanted to do that. But, to learn to run with a partner and then in lead position were huge accomplishments. I was pretty proud of myself, and I knew my mom was absolutely delighted with me and for me.

It had been a wonderful summer, training with my brothers and my father. I had loved every minute of my stay at the kennel. My father, Sandman, and granddad, Argie, both had been "superstars" in their day and were now retired from running in the world-famous Iditarod Sled Dog Race. It wasn't as hard for me to leave this time. I knew my brothers would run in sled dog races and probably even the Iditarod. I would go home to pull my mom and her friends on my sled. Though my heart was happy being with my family, I was missing the children in my mom's classroom. I was looking forward to going to school again. It seemed like I was leading two lives. Is this what it might be like for an Alaskan sled dog to live a double life?

Chapter VIII
Mom and Our Travels

My mom liked to talk to adults and students about the Iditarod Sled Dog Race, and since I was an Alaskan sled dog and now trained to know the trail commands, she decided to take me with her whenever she made the presentations. I loved riding in the car, and I fit perfectly with my fanny on the backseat, my front legs straddling the hump on the floor, and my head poked between the driver and passenger seats. I could look out the front window as Mom drove, and she always talked to me as we zoomed along. Sometimes she had the radio on, but I liked it best when she talked. We traveled many, many miles together, and we even spent some nights in a motel. When she did the presentations, she took all my trail gear and would put it on me. She had a spiffy harness that was put over my head and fit down my body, booties for my feet, a fleece coat that wrapped around my neck and belly, a leg wrap, and a padded winter slip collar that was blue. Mom still had the pink "Sissy" collar from my first summer of training and liked to tell the story of how I had to wear it in front of my brothers. I close my eyes when I hear *that* story.

Mom would hook me onto a piece of gangline so everyone

could see how dogs were hooked up to pull a sled. I would then show everyone how I learned to run/trot in the space. At some places I was even able to be a "show-off" and did my "gee,gee" and "haw,haw" as I walked around the room and turned right or left. Then I would go into my obedience routine of doing the sit, stay, down, come commands, which left folks with their mouths open and saying, "*Wow*, what a smart and well-trained dog!"

Some of the people I have met I will never forget. At the end of a library presentation a man who looked like a granddaddy seemed to want me to visit with him. I found my way across the room, and as I approached him I noticed he had the kindest and gentlest eyes. When he petted me his hands always went the right direction so my fur didn't get pushed up or swirled around. Some people instinctively know how a dog likes to be petted! He even found my most favorite spot to be scratched, no, not behind my ears, although that feels really good too. He put his hands under my chin and gave me scratches that sent me over the moon!

My eyes began to close and I felt myself headed to dreamland, but I knew I couldn't let that happen. I shook myself out of my blissful moment for I knew Mom expected me to walk around and greet everyone. I do not give kisses very freely but because the kind and gentle man had known exactly what I liked, I felt a "thank you" kiss on his cheek was necessary. I planted a nice wet kiss on his cheek, turned quickly, and continued to enjoy myself as I "worked" the room and met all the other people. On the way home Mom casually mentioned that she saw me kiss a stranger. She said she had gone to him and told him it was highly unusual for me to kiss strangers. She also said that she told him I must have felt a special connection. She then said that he said he had been to Alaska many times and had ridden his motorcycle all over the state. He said he was feeling a little sad because he was now too old to return there or to ride his motorcycle, but he had vivid memories he kept stored in his mind. He said he was so happy he had come to see us because it brought all his own memories back to life. Hearing what Mom said made *me* very happy. No wonder I picked him out in the crowd; he loved Alaska, and he loved sled dogs! Mom always says it is important for us to touch someone's life, and I believe we touched each other's lives that day. I will never forget him.

One school that I think was the most magical place for me was the school for the deaf. Mom was passionate about speaking to students at schools, and folks at libraries, social clubs, and retirement facilities while I was delighted with all the attention I was given. My mom was especially thrilled to be at this school, and I felt her excitement. As she spoke to her audience, a person with hearing stood near her and used sign language to tell the audience all the things she was saying. The room was absolutely quiet except for Mom talking. I had to be especially well-behaved. You could tell the children loved all that she was talking about from the looks on their faces. When she said something funny, which she did a lot, they would smile, raise their hands, and twist them back and forth. That was the sign that they thought it was funny and were laughing!

As Mom finished, I spotted a squirrel outside a long wall of floor to ceiling windows. I don't know what possessed me, but I ran to the window, and the squirrel began to run down the long wall of windows on the outside. I knew he was teasing me, but I couldn't help myself and began to run with him. The only trouble was I was on the inside, and he was on the outside! The kids all thought this was hysterical, so they raised and twisted their hands really fast. It was all great fun until the squirrel decided to run away. Then I had to settle myself down and be good again. Mom decided I should do all my obedience commands with her just using hand signals. I thought this was absolutely perfect, for I could show all these kids that I knew sign language too. I puffed out my chest and held my tail high as Mom put me through my obedience paces. She *only* used her hands and no voice. I sat, I went into a down, I stayed, I came to her, I stopped midway coming to her, I walked on her left side, and I never took my eyes off her. I knew exactly what she wanted me to do. I could have done it for hours. The audience was amazed and proud that I knew sign language. That was a very, very special trip, and, again, one I will never, ever forget.

Actually all my trips were special, but the best part was us traveling together and having so many wonderful adventures. We have been all around the Midwest, all the way to the East Coast and the Atlantic Ocean. I didn't really like the salt water in the ocean because it burned my eyes and tasted awful. The waves tried to knock me over, and the crabs tried to pinch my feet. I did attempt to swim in it for a very short time, but my fur got sticky from the salt, and it made me itchy. Mom loved the ocean. I was happy for her, but I didn't care if I visited an ocean ever again!

My favorite place was in Eagle Harbor, Michigan. I loved swimming in Lake Superior, running on the beach, and dashing into the water looking at shiny rocks on the bottom. The water was so clean, cold, and perfect to drink. *No salt!* Mom and I made many trips there and stayed in a good friend's cottage right on the lake. I had super fun climbing on big rocks along the shoreline. I always looked for a flat rock to lie down on and take a snooze as the cool breeze tickled my ears and the sunshine warmed my fur. I love when we take trips back there.

After all my presentations, schooling, and travels, there was now no doubt in my mind that I was in Indiana leading the double life of a sled dog!

Chapter IX
How Could She?

The years flew by, and my life was quiet at home, lively at human school, delightful at my mom's presentations, and adventurous when we travelled. It was all pretty wonderful. I enjoyed taking naps whenever I wanted, and I adored going on walks and then having my free run time. Although my back legs seemed to be getting a little stiff as I was getting older and it took me more time to get into a "sit," I was born to run, so the desire never left my heart. Maybe I wasn't running quite as fast as I did when I was a young pup, but I continued to feel the excitement and happiness when I always ran free. Though I enjoyed my life as an older, smarter, and certainly more mature dog, little did I know how much my life was about to change!

How could she, how could she do this to me? I had always been her one and only. Then one horrible day she brought home this ratty, smelly, dirty ball of fur. There were two eyes deep in the fur, and there was a tail that was longer than the fur ball's entire body. What a mess this thing was! I watched as my mom bathed "it" in the kitchen sink; all the while I was secretly hoping it would disappear down the drain. After the bath and towel drying, as I listened to the cooing and aahing of my mom, I had this horrible feeling that the fur ball was going to stay in *my* home. Why, especially why now? Mom put the puppy down, and she, yes it's a girl, ran right over to me and leaped onto my back. That surprised me and made me angry. I growled at her! My mom quickly said, "Now Annui, *you be a good girl*." I knew at that moment my leisurely life had changed drastically. But I also knew that I did *not* have to like it!

Mom explained to me that she had gotten the puppy from the animal shelter. The puppy needed a good home, since the owner couldn't take care of her. She said it would be nice if I acted like a big sister to her. That meant I would have to teach her things and take care of her. What a horrible request and thought! At that moment I didn't want that ratty fur ball to even come near me, and Mom wanted me to take care of her? I did not want that "thing" to turn *my* world upside down. I decided that I would ignore the horrid fur ball, distance myself from her, and growl at her if she ever came near. That worked initially. Then I realized she would be outside in the backyard playing and having lots of fun, while I would be moping in the house not having any fun at all. I began going out the doggie door to see what was going on, but as soon as the little "Brat" darted toward me I would run back inside. To top off being told I had to be nice, Mom gave her a special name too, "SootFa." This means Snow Flower. I decided to just call her Goofie Soofie because she certainly was goofie, goofie looking and goofie acting! Her tail was so much longer than her body that it acted like a rudder. Whatever direction it pointed that was the way she went. Needless to say, she went sideways most of the time and tumbled head over feet! I actually had some good snickers and snorts when I saw her stumbling and tumbling about.

It didn't take long for Goofie Soofie to grow in size, and I began wondering how big she was going to get. I knew she was *not* an Alaskan sled dog like my brothers and me, but I didn't know what she was. I overheard my mom tell a friend that Goofie Soofie was a Leonberger. The Leonberger breed is a mix of Great Pyrenees, Saint Bernard, and Newfoundland, all *big* dogs. Oh *my*! The days of me being the biggest dog were numbered. I began thinking that perhaps I would have to change my attitude and just accept that ragtag, bratty puppy. But I would still be the boss, the alpha. Maybe, just maybe, it would be fun to teach the pup the obedience and trail commands that I knew.

This was a scary thought, but I began to think that it might be nice to have a partner to pull the sled. I knew Goofie Soofie liked me, for she always wanted to be exactly where I was and to do exactly what I was doing. She would lean into me and even clean my ears. She knew I was the alpha, and she was very much okay with that. What a good thing!

After many months of struggling to accept the now very *large* fur ball, I finally decided it was okay to have her in my home and living with me. Soofie, I no longer call her Goofie Soofie because she is so much bigger than I am, has begun to add to my happiness. We have become great buddies. I am happy she is part of our family. I even let her sleep in my bed, as we switch beds during the night, but she *cannot* sleep in my favorite chair. Soofie is okay with that because she is way too big for it anyway. When she goes to the groomer, I actually miss her and her annoying ways. We ride together in Mom's car, although she takes up much more room than I do. We share chewy toys, and sometimes, to tease her, I take one that she has been chewing on and run away with it. I don't *really* want it, and I don't even like to chew it after she's been gnawing on it. She will come and get it from me, and I gladly let her take it! It's our way of playing together. She never,

ever growls and never gets upset about anything. If I must have a little sister, and I had wished for one many years ago, Soofie is the best giant little sister any dog could have. I was not nice to her for quite a while, and I am sorry for that. But I was a little afraid my mom would love her more than me. I was jealous, and I was being selfish.

When we take walks I am still *always* out in front and Soofie is six steps behind me. I am the lead dog and worked hard learning that position, so everyone should be well aware of that! I trot proudly at a brisk gait with my head held high, my mom and Soofie trailing behind. Soofie doesn't want to be a lead dog, even though I have already taught her all the trail and obedience commands. We have had great fun pulling the sled together, and even though she isn't Wanda, Soofie is still fun to run beside. She certainly can pull hard, but I am still faster than she is because I am an Alaskan sled dog weighing about sixty pounds. She weighs about fifty pounds more than me and would never be able to run in the Iditarod Sled Dog Race, because she is just too, too big. However, she is as sweet and gentle as she is big, and I must confess that *"I love her!"* I realize now it is comforting and quite special to have another furry friend to live with. I would not have said this before, but I think Mom and I should include Soofie when we have our little adventures. She *is* fun to ride in the car with, as long as she gives me plenty of room and lets *me* sit and look out the front window! We are all happy together, and I never think "how could she?" anymore, for it is such fun having Soofie as part of our family.

Epilogue

Life is back to normal, as much as it will ever be. I can take lovely naps throughout the day. Soofie never barks, so the house is very quiet. We all go to Mom's presentations together, and I now have a best friend to play, walk, and run with. I know my mom doesn't love her more than she loves me. I wouldn't tell Soofie this because I would not want to hurt her feelings, but every night before Mom goes to bed she comes to my bed to hug and kiss me. She tells me that I will always be special since we have had so many wonderful years together living my double life. She talks about the times that she took care of my brothers and me at the kennel. She tells me she is very, very, *very* proud of all I have accomplished. Mom took me from my Alaskan home to live with her in Indiana, yet she allowed me to be who I am, an Alaskan sled dog from an Iditarod racing family. She and I have developed an incredible bond over the years, and I was silly to think that Soofie would cause that to change. Mom's heart is filled with a huge amount of love, which she generously gives to both of us.

I have learned some important things because of Soofie living with us. There could be another fur brother or sister added to our family, and it would absolutely be okay. Moms always embrace, care for, and love however many may join a family. Moms seem to be like that in human families as well as in fur families! Just as I am special to Mom in certain ways, Soofie is special in her own ways. I learned that sharing can be fun, and to have another "fur ball" to play with is pretty wonderful. I miss my Soofie when we are not together, and I know she feels the same way. I can't wait until the winter comes again so that Soofie and I can dash through the cold, powdery snow once again pulling happy, laughing children on the sled. Things are easier and more fun to do when you have a partner. I am so very glad to have Soofie as my running mate!

It is also nice to have a buddy who helps me try and chase the rabbits, chipmunks, and squirrels when we are running free. Since I can't run as fast as I used to, Soofie is a great partner when we try to outrun those critters. I am usually aware that they are near way before Soofie ever is because she likes to look at the sky, birds, and butterflies, while I have my nose to the ground and am constantly picking up scents. She knows I have tracked something interesting because I pick up my "sniffing" pace. Finally Soofie will get involved. She has really good eyesight, so after I have picked up the scent she stops, looks in the distance, spots the critter, and then takes off like a rocket. I watch her run like the wind, knowing she is having the best time, and I happily follow behind at a nice, easy trot. Once again we have worked together, and it is the best feeling ever. No, we never catch the critters, but that is not really important. Just being together, running free, and having fun makes the "chasing" adventures all worthwhile. It's so nice having a buddy!

I am certain my mom and Soofie will continue developing their relationship based on loyalty and trust. I now understand and am proud and happy to say that my mom is "our" mom. Soofie deserves to be loved and treasured just as much as I am. I predict the three of us will continue to live a wonderful life together filled with many more adventures in the future! I may wake up tomorrow morning and find we are headed off on another trip, or we may be off to a school or library, or we may visit a person who isn't feeling well and needs some doggie love, or we may head to a fun park to see other dogs and people, or we may have a day to rest at home and just enjoy being together, Soofie, Mom, and me.

When I take my many naps, I dream of my family, my school days, my trail and obedience training, my presentations, my travels, and, of course, my Soofie and our mom. The combination of my life in Alaska and my life in Indiana make it incredibly exciting and special to be an Alaskan sled dog that is definitely living a double life!

Glossary

Alaskan husky—A mixed-breed husky bred for endurance and racing performance.

booties—Paw coverings to protect a sled dog's feet. Made of Cordura fabric or fleece, strapped on by Velcro.

bunkhouse—Cabin where kennel workers live.

canine school—Schooling that trains dogs and owners in obedience commands and agility.

four-wheeler—Small, gas-operated, four-wheeled open vehicle.

gangline/tow line—Main cabled line that runs forward from the sled. All dogs are connected to the gangline or towline by other lines.

gee—Command for right turn.

harness—System of webbing worn by a sled dog that distributes the pulled weight evenly across its shoulders and back.

haw—Command for left turn.

Iditarod Sled Dog Race—A 1,049-mile marathon sled dog race across Alaska from the city of Anchorage to the town of Nome. The "Super Bowl" of long-distance racing.

Inupiaq—Eskimos who live along the Arctic Ocean and Chuckchi Sea.

kennel—A group of dogs owned by a musher. May also describe where the dogs live.

lead—A long strap that hooks to a dog's collar when walking; also called a leash.

lead dog—An intelligent and fast dog that runs in front of the others at the head of the team.

leg wrap—Elastic fabric wrapped around a dog's tendons to prevent postracing swelling.

musher—Driver of a sled.

neckline—A short line connecting a dog's collar to the gangline. It can also be between the two collars of a double lead.

overflow—Water that is on top of frozen ice because the ice has gotten so thick it pushes water up and over the ice.

swing dog—A dog that runs directly behind the leader. His/her job is to "swing" the team in the turns or curves.

team dog—Any dog other than the leader, swing, or wheel dog.

tug—Loop at the end of the harness that the tugline is hooked to.

tugline—Line that connects the dog's harness to the gangline or towline.

veterinarian—A person trained and authorized to treat animals medically.

wheel dog—A dog placed directly in front of the sled/four-wheeler. His/her job is to "pull" the sled out and around corners or trees.

yearling—An animal that is one year old or has not completed its second year.

Made in the USA
Lexington, KY
25 March 2017